ENLIGHTENMENT

BRUCE GOLDEN

Published by Water Dragon Publishing
waterdragonpublishing.com

ISBN 978-1-962538-37-4 (Trade Paperback)

FIRST EDITION

10 9 8 7 6 5 4 3 2 1

ENLIGHTENMENT

THEY'D BEEN HUNTING HIM SINCE SUNRISE — four vague shapes on horseback — always skirting the horizon, always looming ominously. He didn't know if they were part of the marauding band that had thundered into his community or not. All he knew was running. He'd run when they first attacked — when he saw Will Landesgard cut down with a long metal shaft that shimmered in the moonlight as it struck. He'd run and he'd hid, fear an acrid scent in his nostrils, and then he'd run some more. How long he'd run, he wasn't certain. How long he slept, collapsed with fatigue, hidden in a patch of scrub, he had no idea. *How much time had passed? A day? Two? How many sunrises had there been?*

At one point, Konner thought he'd escaped, but then he'd seen the four riders in the distance — four menacing silhouettes posed against a backdrop of his own panic. So he ran again. When he was too exhausted to run any more, when his legs gave out, his lungs burned, and his feet cried out in pain, he'd found another place to hide. Not that there were many places to hide on that hilly plain. He picked the best place he could find and lay flat, unmoving, as still as the Harvest Christ prepared for planting.

When he couldn't hold his eyes open any longer, he found himself awash in a chaotic dream. Everywhere he turned, his people were under attack. He saw his father butchered like a hog, his mother attacked, his little sister Hazel scooped up like a frightened animal, roughly bound and slung over the back of a horse. When she screamed, he woke with a start.

Try as he might to sort through the horrific images, Konner couldn't remember. *Had it actually happened like that? Was it only a dream, his imagination, or had he seen it all with his own eyes?*

He sat up and looked around. There they were — the four horsemen — still a ways behind him, mounted on a hill as if surveying the terrain, no doubt searching for him. Konner thought he saw one of them point in his direction. One of the horses reared up and they all started down the hill toward him.

He surged to his feet and ran.

He ran as fast as he could, slowing only once to glance backwards. He no longer saw his pursuers, only an uneven terrain studded with high brush and endless cacti. He turned his eyes ahead just in time to feel the loss of contact. He'd taken to the air, and for a brief second Konner thought he was flying. He wasn't flying. He was falling — falling off the edge of an eroded bank. He flailed the air in vain and landed hard, his left knee crashing against a rocky outcropping. The pain was unlike anything he'd experienced. He curled fetal-like, grabbed hold of the knee, and tried to muffle his cries of agony.

He lay there for a long while, unwilling to test his injury — afraid to move. He kept expecting the riders to come upon him and put an end to the pain. He was resigned to it — almost welcomed it. After a time, when no one came, he imagined they must have ridden by him. He decided to test his leg. It didn't take long to discover he could put no weight on it at all. The knee had already begun to swell.

He needed something to lean on. He tried hopping, but instead fell back into the dust and whimpered in pain. He knew he was going nowhere, so he rolled onto his back and lay there, staring at the sky. He reached into his pocket and felt his lucky goldstone. It was still there — for all the good it had done him. He began to wonder if it was lucky at all. He wondered about a lot of things that were ... and things that were no longer.

When a sudden wind kicked up with intense fury, he turned his head and shielded his eyes. After it passed, he opened them and stared straight ahead. Not more than six paces from him lay an ancient-looking corpse, as desiccated as the sand which blanketed it. Part skeleton, part dusty leather, he wasn't sure if it had been a man or a woman. The initial shock of seeing it there, so close to him, gave him the shiver-tingles and made him want to get up and run. He tried, but could only shriek in pain. So he just lay there staring at it, wondering who it might have been, and what kind of life he or she might have lived.

It wasn't long before he heard the sound of horses. Desperately he tried to crawl into the shade of a scrawny bush where he thought he might hide. Then he held his breath.

"What have we here, Banshee?"

The voice was so near, Konner knew he'd been discovered. He scrambled to sit up.

He saw no horses and only one man. An old man — at least as old as his gramps had been before he got put in the south field. He even had white hair and a scraggly white beard like Gramps. Konner had to blink twice to be sure it *wasn't* Gramps. Of course, it couldn't be.

This old fellow wore a hat with a wide brim and a dimpled crown. It was dusty brown in color — or covered with desert dust — he wasn't sure which. He didn't look like one of those raiders, but Konner couldn't be sure. Not that there was much he could do about it. He couldn't run any more.

"I heard you cry out, boy," said the old fellow. "What's wrong with you?"

Konner stayed silent.

The stranger stepped closer and looked down at him with penetrating silver-grey eyes. "You think he doesn't speak English, Banshee?"

Konner wondered why the fellow spoke as if he were talking to someone else, and then saw the little animal sitting off to his right, a few feet away. It was akin to a skinny rabbit, but with shorter legs and ears, and a longer tail. Its thick fur was a patchwork of gray and orange. It just sat there staring at him. He half-expected the strange creature to answer the old fellow.

"*Habla Español? Neoneun hangug malhani?* I see lights on, Banshee, but it doesn't appear anybody's home." He bent down and took a closer look at Konner's leg. "That knee doesn't look so good. How'd you manage that?"

Konner looked back to the old man and blurted out, "They were chasing me. Four of them, on horses. They — a bunch of them — attacked our home, killed my ..."

The old man looked at him with an expression that melded both concern and skepticism. He turned and with surprising vigor, clambered up the nearest hill. Konner could see him turn and look in every direction.

When he came down, he said to Konner, "I don't see any riders. Whatever happened, you're safe now." He turned to the animal. "Well, Banshee, I guess we can't just leave him here."

The little furry beast rose from its haunches and whipped its tail about as if in response.

"What's your name, boy?"

Konner hesitated, but when he couldn't think of a reason not to respond, he said, "Konner ... Konner Grainwell."

"Alright, Konner Grainwell, let's get you up and over to my wagon."

•　　　•　　　•

The stranger's wagon was larger than any Konner's folk had used for harvesting, and it was enclosed like a little square house. The house part was painted with peculiar swirls and symbols, and blotches of various bright colors. Inside it was packed with things he could only guess at. Pulling the wagon were two horses the likes of which astounded Konner. They were rust-colored, tall and brawny — much bigger and more muscular than any horse he'd seen. When he wanted them to get going, the old man called the horses by their names — Dodge and Durango.

Those weren't the only animals the fellow had with names. There was that funny long-tailed rabbit he called Banshee, and three more of the little critters waiting for him at the wagon. Konner wondered about them, but didn't say anything until he'd managed, with the old guy's help, to get up on the wagon's seat. His knee still hurt real bad. It hurt like the time he stepped barefoot in some cook fire ash that was still burning.

Up on the seat, the Banshee creature sat between them, while two of the other little beasts stayed back in the wagon. The third one, doing what seemed impossible, went right up the side of the wagon in a flash of leaps, all the way to the top when the old man called out, "Frodo, up high!"

"He's the best damn lookout there is," he said when he saw Konner's astonishment.

"What kind of funny rabbits are those?"

"They're not rabbits, they're cats," he replied. "Haven't you ever seen a cat?"

Konner shook his head.

"Well, I guess maybe you wouldn't have. There aren't many still around, though I once met a fellow who had dozens of them, and names for each one."

"Do yours have names?"

"Sure — of course. You met Banshee there, sitting next to you. The chubby black and white one is Bilbo. The gold one up top is Frodo, and that scrawny all black one is Gollum."

Konner thought the names were strange, but he didn't say so. He did wonder about them though. Horses were work animals, but cats?

"What do they do, these cats?" he asked. "Do you eat them?"

"Eat them?" The stranger's response exploded from his lips, then he burst out laughing. "Of course I don't eat them," he said, still chuckling. "They're my friends — my traveling companions. Oh, now and again they'll catch a rodent or a lizard and bring it to me. If it's big enough I might even cook it. But their only job is to keep me company."

Konner never heard of anyone keeping company with any kind of animal. That's what people were for. Of course, the old guy *was* all alone — maybe even touched in the head a bit.

"So where are you from, Konner Grainwell?"

Konner looked around at the landscape, at the overhead sun, and realized he was no longer certain which way was home.

"I ... don't know. I'm ... not sure."

"How long since you left there?"

"Uh, two days ... I think."

"You think? It must have been a rough time if you're not sure. You said some men attacked your village — men on horseback. How many men?"

Konner shrugged.

"What *do* you remember?"

Konner didn't respond right away, but when he did there was a hint of anger in his voice.

"Fire ... blood. They were killing folks, burning things. It was ..." He turned and looked away from the old man.

The stranger didn't ask any more questions — didn't say anything else until they stopped for the night in a small grove of palm trees. Until then, they rode in silence, though Konner's thoughts were anything but tranquil. They were populated with flashes of carnage, a cacophony of screams, and shadows he didn't want to discern. Instead he tried, without much success, *not* to remember.

•   •   •

They never came upon any horsemen, any people from his community, or the community itself. Konner guessed they were traveling in the wrong direction, though which way was the right direction he couldn't tell. He knew the sun rose in the east, set in the west, and thereby knew which ways were north and south, but that didn't help him. He'd been so panicked when he'd run, he'd never bothered to keep track. He ran much of the first night, and likely hadn't gone in a straight line.

As the first twilight in the company of the old man approached, they stopped and the stranger spent some time unhitching his horses before helping Konner down. Konner's knee still hurt when he put any weight on it, so his new companion fashioned him a crutch from an old tree limb. Soon they were sitting near a fire the old fellow had built. He ate what he was given — something that seemed part bread, part weed. It was peculiar but filling, and his stomach had been empty for some time.

He watched the stranger, his odd little animals sitting next to and all around him, wondering where the fellow had come from — how he'd ended up out here all alone.

"Have you ever been to Faraway?" Konner asked, breaking the silence.

The old guy looked at him. "Where?"

"Faraway. My gramps used to tell me stories about Faraway. I wondered if you came from there, or ever went there."

"I don't know of any place with such a name, though I've journeyed far and wide, wandered off the beaten track, taken the road less traveled, and rambled through no man's land." He smiled as if he'd said something funny, then paused for a few seconds to think. "No, can't say that I've been there, though I've certainly roved here, there, and just about everywhere."

"You mean you're not really going anywhere — any certain place?"

"Ah, not all those who wander are lost," he replied with a smug look. "All journeys have destinations, even if the traveler isn't aware of them."

Konner wasn't sure the man's words made any sense. *How could you not expect to end up where you go?* He decided that's what he needed to do right then was to go relieve himself. He stood with some difficulty and a fair amount of pain, got his crutch under him, and turned to walk away from the fire. As he did, the crutch knocked against something laying nearby on the ground.

"Careful there!" exclaimed the old fellow, jumping up and hurrying over to the fire. He plucked something from the flames and quickly doused the embers on it that had begun to smoke. "You almost burned this, boy. We've lost too many to fire already."

Konner could see the old guy was upset, though he wasn't certain why. He didn't even know what the thing was, though this fellow acted as if it were something precious.

"I'm … sorry."

"It's okay," he said calmly. "No harm done. But a book will burn pretty quick when it gets going. Then all those words will be gone forever."

"Book?"

"Yeah, *this* book. I was going to read some later." The stranger looked at him, realization dawning. "You don't know what a book is — do you?"

Konner shook his head.

"Hell's bells, boy, you've got a lot to learn."

"What is a *book*?"

"A book is ... well a book is the purest essence of a human soul — the soul who wrote it. Books are the quietest and most constant of friends — the most accessible and wisest of counselors — the most patient of teachers."

"How does it do all that?"

"How? Well,,," He stopped as if he didn't know how to respond, scratched at the beard on his face, then gathered himself. "You don't know how to read, do you?"

Konner shook his head. "Well, books are for reading. They can be entertaining — full of wonderment and adventure — or they can be about truth — about what happened, how and why. Books are full of words — you know what words are?"

Konner nodded.

"A book is a bunch of words written in the proper order to describe something, teach something, or just tell a story. Here, look at this book you almost kicked in the fire. What's the color you see here on its cover?"

Konner could see, even by the firelight, that it looked like a bunch of trees and was mostly one color. "Green," he said.

"Okay, you know the word green. Well, there are a group of letters — symbols — which make up the word *green*. You see this at the top of the book. These are all letters. They make up words. The name of this book is actually like two words put together."

He covered half the letters with his hand. "You see this word? This is how you write *green* using these symbols. If you wanted to describe the color of this book as green, you'd write it like this." He moved his hand to cover the portion that read "green."

"Now this part of the word says *Ever*. You know, like if you say, 'The horizon seems to go on forever and ever.' Or if you ask, 'Is that pig ever going to stop eating?' You know what a pig is, right?"

Konner nodded. "Now, if you put the two words together," he said, taking his hand off the book and running a finger under the letters, "it says 'Evergreen'. That's the name of this book — *Evergreen*. The word means something that is always green, like a tree or a bush that's green year-round. Get it?"

Konner's expression mirrored his bafflement.

"I know, it's not easy to understand at first. But words can be powerful things when linked together in the right sequence. Don't worry, I'll teach you to read."

"Why?"

"*Why*?" he echoed with a hint of consternation. "Because reading is knowledge, and knowledge is power. That's why."

"Okay," replied Konner, and limped off to relieve his now powerfully bulging bladder.

· · ·

They were everywhere he turned — wherever he dared look. Terrifying men on horseback, black wraiths with red eyes trampling newly planted fields, brandishing weapons and torches, maiming, killing, burning. He saw the bodies of his father, his mother — even the Trouble Brothers lay bleeding in a ditch, their eyes unmoving but still mocking him. He tried to run, but each way he turned they were there — grinning, grimacing, howling, each face looking every bit like the picture he'd once seen of ol' Demon Drought. No matter how fast he ran, there was no escaping them. He fell, a horse reared over him, a blade glinting in the moonlight rushed down at him …

"Wake up. Wake up, Konner Grainwell. You're safe."

Konner opened his eyes, jerking awake. The old man was leaning over him.

"That must have been quite a nightmare," he said. "But that's all it was."

Konner sat up and looked around. It was sometime after dawn. He saw the wagon, the two unhitched horses grazing, and one of the cat animals, Gollum, looking at him. He realized it had just been another dream. Another horrible dream.

Gollum stopped staring and sauntered under the wagon. Konner watched him go, saw him leap up and disappear. Curious where he could have possibly gone, Konner scooted to where he could see better. There was an opening under the wagon's structure with some kind of sliding door. Fully open, Konner thought he could fit through it. Little Gollum had jumped right through and disappeared inside the wagon.

"That's my cat door … and my escape hatch," said the old man. "You should always have a good escape plan." He winked. "Come on, let's get you something to eat. A little food will fill your belly and put your mind in a good place."

Konner ate what was brought to him without paying much attention to what it was. The truth was, he was trying not to think at all.

Then he blurted out, "I don't know your name. What do I call you?"

"My name?" The stranger seemed momentarily puzzled by the question. He was quiet for a few seconds as if trying to think of an answer — to recall his own name. "You can just call me Teacher, since it looks like you've got a lot to learn."

One thing Konner quickly learned was that Teacher was brimful of words he didn't understand. Even if he knew all the words separately, sometimes the way the old guy put them together made no sense.

Like when he got his first lesson in reading, Teacher said, "A journey of a thousand miles must begin with a single step." Yet they weren't going anywhere. They were just sitting there next to the wagon. And when Konner hesitated to try and read his first word because it seemed all those words were going to be too much for him, Teacher said, "The secret to getting ahead is getting started." Konner didn't know what *head* he was talking about, or why he'd want a head. Was he talking about Konner's head?

•　　　•　　　•

The howling of the sandstorm had been so furious, it made Konner think of the Coriolis storms he read about in the book *Dune*. Even though it had been hard to read, it was his favorite ... so far, and Paul Muad'Dib was his favorite character, because he too, had been thrown into a world he knew nothing of. That's what Konner felt like every time he picked up a new book. All the pages, all the words were a new world he'd never visited.

The sandstorm passed before midday, and before long the sky settled on its habitual blue, dotted with a motley patchwork of clouds. A short time later, Konner noticed there was no wind at all, and the horizon in all directions was as silent and serene as a pool of shallow water. It was as though the passing storm had pacified the harshness of the landscape. Nature's wrath and nature's calm divided by a handful of heartbeats.

Konner didn't know exactly how long he'd been with Teacher — how many holidays he'd missed — but it had been long enough that he'd grown some. He realized one day that he no longer had the planting, the caring, and the harvesting to mark time. He was also aware that he no longer wondered about his family or his previous home. They were a distant, though still painful, memory. A place he'd left behind, untold miles back. Home was now wherever Durango and Dodge took them. Home was just over the next rise. Home was in the pages of the next book.

Teacher had dozens of books, and on a rare occasion they found new ones. Konner had only read about half of them, and only fully understood half of those. But he could read them all now — only once having to ask Teacher what a certain word meant.

Once the storm passed, and they exited the shelter of the wagon, Konner propped himself up against its shady side. Gollum and Banshee curled up next to him as he read *The Complete Poems, Lyrics, and Musings of James Douglas Morrison*.

It wasn't easy. He found poetry, often times, was the hardest thing to understand — even if it had the fewest words. Teacher said that a poem was usually less about information, and more about the images it formed in your mind or the emotions it forged in your gut.

Konner found this Morrison fellow to have some strange images, and some even stranger ideas — at least what he could understand of them. So much of what he read was set in a strange, outlandish kind of world — a dead world he'd never known. It was hard for him to picture highways packed with mechanical automobiles or cities with millions of people. Some of things he read about — the devices, the cultures — were difficult for him to even imagine. Yet Teacher told him these things were real, and not just flights of fancy.

Konner looked up from his reading when Dodge suddenly whinnied and stomped his right front hoof a couple of times. It looked as if the horse was counting. It was unusual enough that Konner put his book down and stood to have a look around. Teacher had gone off with Durango to look for water. The horse had a good nose for it and had saved them from dying of thirst more than once. Frodo and Bilbo had tagged along, though they had no particular skill at finding anything other than the occasional lizard.

Konner didn't see anything on the horizon, though he did wonder about Teacher. He'd been gone quite a while. He was about to sit back down with his book when Frodo scampered into their camp. He was breathing hard, as if he'd run quite a distance. Gollum and Banshee raised up to peek at him through sleepy cat eyes as well. Konner looked in the direction the cat had come from, but he didn't see anything unusual.

He didn't think much of it — the cats were always running about wherever they wanted. He propped himself against the wagon wheel again and was about to pick up his book when Frodo walked over to him and cried out in a way Konner had never heard. It was definitely strange — strange enough that Konner took hold of the cat and looked him over to see if he was injured.

He seemed alright, but when Konner put him back down, he cried again, and ran off in the direction he'd come from. He was acting just peculiar enough that Konner decided to follow him.

His knee had healed long ago, but on occasion it still bothered him. Some days it was fine and he could run like the wind, and other days, especially when it was damp and cloudy, it nagged him with its aching. Today there were storm clouds on the horizon, and he could feel a twinge as he walked across the uneven ground of the sandy mesa that was their current home.

It wasn't too long before he saw Durango in the distance, but no sign of Teacher. He also saw, off in another direction, the signs of an ant migration. There were thousands of them traveling together in a massive column. They looked like a dark red river. He got the shiver-tingles just seeing them.

Konner had learned that such a river brought only death with it. Teacher made certain they traveled far out of their way to avoid such a migration, and whenever he came across a singular ant — a scout he called it — he'd be sure and kill it. He didn't want the scout leading the rest back to wherever he and Konner were at.

Konner was worried. The ants were too close. They needed to pack up and move on. He had to find Teacher right away.

As Konner got closer to the horse he finally spotted Teacher, lying on the ground.

"Flies and fleas!" he exclaimed as he broke into a run, despite the pain in his knee. He quickly knelt next to Teacher, who seemed asleep but began convulsing, his body as wildly agitated as an animal in the throes of death. In fact, Konner thought Teacher must be dying to act so. He didn't know what else to do, so he tried to restrain Teacher's movements. Shortly, the convulsions stopped and Teacher opened his eyes.

"What ..." he asked, dazed and disoriented.

"Are you alright?" asked Konner. "You were shaking something awful."

"Yes, I'll be okay in a minute. Just let me gather myself."

"What is it? What's wrong?"

"Don't worry. It's something I've lived with for a long time. It's a disease that only flares up on occasion."

Konner looked more worried than ever. "A disease?"

"Don't worry, I'll be fine. And you can't catch it. It's something I was born with — called epilepsy."

"Are you sure you're okay?"

"I will be. Hand me my hat and help me up now. We still have to find some water."

"I don't think we have time. The ants are on the march."

•   •   •

It wasn't what Konner expected. Of course, he didn't know what to expect. When they approached the large settlement, Konner had been anxious to see other people. It had been a while since they'd seen anyone else, and they'd never come across a place as populated as this one seemed to be.

He was surprised by the wary, suspicious eyes with which the townspeople regarded them. An old man and a boy shouldn't have looked dangerous, but you wouldn't have known it by the inhospitable stares aimed their way. Many of the residents didn't even come outside. They peered from openings in their gaunt domiciles to get a safe look at the strangers. Their reactions spoke volumes about their previous encounters with outsiders.

Konner could tell by the well-kept fields which surrounded the hamlet that it was a farming community much like the one he grew up in, though his recollection of his old home was as hazy as the horizon. This one was larger and, in his mind, the first real town he'd ever seen. They'd come upon small encampments and what he thought of as little villages many times. But he thought of this new place as a town — maybe because of all the books he'd been reading and the line of gutted, decrepit old buildings that formed its center. It *looked* like what he pictured a town should look like.

Teacher said these places were the seeds of a new civilization, but Konner wasn't so sure. There didn't seem very much new about them. Like this one, they were often constructed upon the relics of the world that once existed, but now few could remember. Ancient brick walls were conjoined with those constructed of newer adobe, and roofs were patched with a variety of scraps, material from both now and then.

Teacher had long ago told him about how the old world ended — about what he and his people used to call the "rainfire." It was indeed a rain of fire that had scorched the entire world ... at least as far as Teacher knew, and he'd been there to live through it. He said he once figured out how many days it had been since the end of everything, and reckoned there were about 20,000 of them. Konner had never heard of such a number, but he knew it was a lot more than he could count.

Here and there in the town, Konner saw the cross signs. It wasn't the first time he'd seen such, but he'd never seen so many. Teacher had told him all about the story of God and Jesus, and he knew that so many crosses meant these were a god-fearing people. From what he knew, he still wasn't sure why people feared this God person. Teacher said it was a complicated subject he'd learn more about as he read more. He did know there was something in this religion thing similar to the Harvest Christ his own people had celebrated. Teacher told him the Jesus character was also known as the Christ. How it all worked, Konner wasn't sure yet.

Once they got over their suspicions, the people started coming over and talking with Teacher. They paid special attention to Dodge and Durango, and Konner noted that he hadn't seen any other horses in the town. A handful of children came out to stare at the giant beasts, but were soon distracted by the cats resting aboard the wagon. When Bilbo began sniffing at Banshee's hindquarters, she took exception and smacked him with her paw. That prompted several laughs, and the children giggled amongst themselves.

Teacher learned that the last time a pack of bandits had come through, they'd taken all the town's horses ... among other things. So, he worked out a trade, where they got some food in exchange for letting the townspeople borrow the horses, under his supervision, for some hauling work. And, as he often did, Teacher offered them other things he'd found in his travels to make more trades. He called them *doodads* and *gewgaws.*

When they finally settled down for the night at one end of the town, Konner built a fire to cook the meat they'd gotten in trade. Teacher didn't tell him what kind of meat it was and he didn't ask. They hadn't had much lately so he wasn't going to *look a gift horse in the mouth* — an expression Teacher liked to use. Konner wasn't sure why anyone would want to look in a horse's mouth. He'd done it once, and what he saw wasn't pretty.

"That was good," said Teacher when he finished his meal. "Not as good as chocolate, but close."

"What's chocolate?"

"Just something I was thinking about from long ago. You've never tasted chocolate, have you? Of course not. You're too young. I remember when there was nothing better than chocolate. The last time I ate a chocolate bar I was still driving around in my Dodge Durango. Must have been close to fifty years back. Found it in a vending machine. If I close my eyes, I think I can still taste it."

Teacher closed his eyes.

"You were driving Dodge and Durango even back then?"

"Not the horses," said Teacher, opening his eyes. "That was when I still had an automobile that ran. It was a Dodge Durango. You've read about automobiles — cars — right?"

Konner nodded.

"I was just a little older than you back then. I met this girl and she … well, that's a story for another time."

Teacher picked up his book, a signal that he was done talking, and rested against the wagon. Frodo, Bilbo,

Banshee, and Gollum had especially appreciated the meat scraps they'd gotten for dinner and were still busily licking their coats clean when Konner and Teacher settled back to read by the firelight. But it was tough to concentrate because they kept hearing a crying noise. Konner had heard such crying before, many times when he was young. He was sure it was a baby in distress.

Finally, exasperated, Teacher closed his book and got up. He set off into the town without a word. Konner decided to follow him. The crying got louder and louder, and finally they found the source of it. It was indeed an infant, and after speaking with the child's mother and father, Teacher marched back to the wagon, mixed together one of his concoctions, cooked it up into soup, and then took it back to the family.

Konner overheard Teacher tell the parents that his "tea" was made of sacred herbs blessed by God himself. He told them how much and how often to give it to the baby. They thanked him and by the time he and Konner had got back to their campsite, the crying had stopped.

It all left Konner confused. It wasn't unusual that Teacher provided someone with some kind of healing ointment or potion. He'd done that before — usually in trade. But he knew Teacher took no stock in God talk or religion, and wondered how he'd gotten herbs that were blessed. When he asked Teacher about it, the old man just sat and picked up his book.

Without looking at Konner he said, "The baby had colic — a common enough ailment. I made a tea out of chamomile and ginger. It should soothe the child's stomach."

"But why did you tell them you used sacred herbs blessed by God? Where would you get such herbs?"

Teacher looked at Konner with mild disappointment. "I've taught you better than to believe in such, boy. You know there's no such things as *sacred* herbs. There's probably not even a god. And if there is, he's got better things to do than spend time blessing dried weeds."

"Then why did you say it?"

"You never contradict someone's superstitions. Sometimes it's better to use those beliefs to help the person ... or yourself. A little hocus pocus never hurt. Don't forget that."

When the baby's parents brought a chicken for Teacher the next day, thanking him for curing their sick child, Konner figured Teacher was right. It was a lesson he promised himself to remember.

•   •   •

Konner had seen many pregnant animals before — mostly livestock — but he thought Banshee looked especially funny. It was as if the cat had swallowed something large and round, making her legs look even skinnier than usual. He wove a basket out of yucca leaves for Banshee to birth her babies in, but every time he put her in it, she wouldn't stay.

"Why doesn't she like the basket?"

"I don't know," said Teacher, "but never try to out-stubborn a cat. Women and cats will do as they please. Men and dogs should relax and get used to it. She'll have her kittens wherever she wants. I'm just glad she's pregnant. I doubt there are many cats left in the world. It wouldn't hurt to have some more."

"Who do you think the father is?"

"Could be anyone of those rascals," said Teacher. "I think they all had a go at her when she was in heat."

Konner remembered the noisy nights when Banshee's suitors came a'calling. He thought they were fighting until Teacher explained what was really going on. It was quite a ruckus, but it broke up the boredom Konner often felt during their endless travels. The desolate, monotonous prairie took its toll on him sometimes. They'd often go weeks without seeing anyone or anything, before coming upon some new settlement. Cats weren't the only thing there weren't many of. People were a rare sight too.

Those folks they *did* find were usually friendly, if a little suspicious at first. It helped that he and Teacher were obviously not much of a threat. They'd trade some of the knickknacks and gewgaws that Teacher had found on their journeys, or he'd offer a potion or salve or some kind of healing herb to someone who was ill. There always seemed to be sick folks, suffering from one malady or another. Usually Teacher could help them with something, even if it was just "giving them a positive attitude" as he liked to say.

It had been weeks since they'd last seen anyone else, and Konner was resting in the shade with his latest book, which he'd recently found in some old ruins. He was fascinated with what he thought of as "the tricks" he read about in *Mindfulness and Hypnosis: The Power of Suggestion to Transform Experience*. Some of them reminded him of how Teacher talked to strangers when he was selling something. But these tricks went beyond that. It seemed, if you knew how, you could get people to do what you wanted them too ... even if they weren't inclined to at first.

It took him some time to appreciate it, but Konner now fervently believed what Teacher had told him long ago, that books were the "wisest of counselors." He relished most of them, and always looked forward to immersing himself in another. To find a new book, as he had this one, was a joyous occasion.

It wasn't just books and the pleasure of reading that Teacher had introduced him to. He'd taught Konner how to live off the land. How to find water, which plants were edible, which ones could cure, and which ones could kill. Konner had learned how to deal with strangers — when to be bold and when to blend in. He was no longer the terrified lost boy he'd been when Teacher first found him. His horizons had been expanded in all the ways that seemed important. He was confident in his knowledge, though his confidence was always tempered by something Teacher once told him. "You're only ignorant of what you don't know."

As he was reading, he heard Teacher climb to the top of the wagon where Frodo and the other cats often lazed in the sun on a cool day. He didn't know why Teacher was up there, and was too taken by his book to find out. But it wasn't long before Teacher called him.

"Konner. Come up here."

Reluctantly, Konner put down his book and made his way onto the wagon's roof.

"What is it?" he asked. But as he spoke, he saw Teacher gesturing toward the western horizon.

Konner shielded his eyes from the sun and looked in the direction Teacher was pointing. What he saw was a massive ant migration. Even though they were far off, he knew it was ants because of its size and the way it flowed across the plain like a gentle river. But there was nothing gentle about a horde of ants. Ants were part of the landstory he'd been taught as a sprout. But this was the largest migration he'd ever seen. He couldn't begin to guess how many millions of ants were on the march. It was an imposing sight.

"Seems like they're always moving. Where do you think they're going?" asked Konner.

"Wherever they want," replied Teacher, still staring into the distance. He watched them for a moment longer. "You know they're much bigger than they used to be."

"Bigger?"

Teacher nodded and said, "When I was a boy, ants were tiny little insects. The biggest ones I ever saw would fit on my fingertip. Now they're the size of crickets, and smarter than they ever were.

"Smarter?"

"That's right. I've watched them over the years, and I'm sure of it. They've changed more than just their size. It has something to do with the bobbin plants."

"That's the bush with the purple berries you use for medicine?"

He nodded. "After the comet hit, the bobbins seemed to flourish, and they definitely attracted the ants. I used to think it was something sweet they must like, but the more I watched, the more the ants changed. I've come to believe it's something else — that somehow the bobbins have had a mutating effect on the ants. What's stranger, is that they protect those plants as if they were protecting their own queen. I once saw a man cut off a bobbin branch loaded with berries instead of just picking some. He was swarmed by ants and dead before he could take a half dozen steps."

"Why did it only happen after the comet?" asked Konner. "You think the comet changed the bobbin plants somehow?"

"Maybe," said Teacher, still staring at the distant migration. "Or maybe it brought the bobbins with it."

•   •   •

Teacher had been ill for many weeks, but in the last few days it had gotten worse. He was having frequent pains in his chest and trouble breathing. When it got so bad he couldn't move around much, Konner made a place for him to lie inside the wagon and asked what he could get him. Teacher said there was nothing that would help. He said he'd tried everything he could think of, but none of his herbs or potions had worked.

"What about some bobbin berries?" asked Konner. "You said they're good for lots of things."

"I don't have any more, and I doubt they'd cure what ails me. This is ... something else."

"But there's a chance — right?" asked Konner. "They *could* cure you. I could go find some more."

"No, no, it's too dangerous. I'm just old, my boy. There's no cure for old age."

Konner had been traveling with Teacher for many years, but he had no idea of his mentor's exact age. He knew he was very old — certainly older than his gramps was when he was planted in the south field. Konner had accepted the death of his gramps as the natural way of things — the way of Holiday and the Harvest Christ — but now he was fearful Teacher might die. Maybe because he'd gotten used to the old fellow — or maybe because of what he learned from Teacher's books. Or maybe because he didn't want to be alone in the world.

"Konner." Teacher called to him from inside the wagon.

Konner hurried to him. Teacher had propped himself up inside the wagon, and was stroking Gollum, who lay on his lap. The cat was very old as well, and not moving around as well as it used to.

"Do you need something?"

"It's hard for me to hold a book up for very long. Would you read to me?"

"What would you like me to read?"

"Anything. Whatever you've been reading."

So, Konner retrieved his current book, *The Wit and Wisdom of Mark Twain*, and sat on one of the storage boxes in the back of the wagon. It wasn't a story book like most of the ones he read. It was filled with short little bits of philosophy and humorous anecdotes. Some of them made sense to Konner, but others belonged to a time and a place he had no reference to.

He began reading out loud, and occasionally Teacher would chuckle. Sometimes he would cough and Konner would get him a drink of water. But Teacher kept telling him to "Go on. Read some more."

Konner continued to read. He didn't stop until it appeared Teacher had fallen asleep. He moved to leave the old man in peace, but then Teacher opened his eyes.

"Did you finish?" he asked.

"No, but I thought maybe you needed to rest."

Teacher nodded. "Help me lie back down."

Konner helped him lie flat, and even with all the squirming around, Gollum didn't move.

"Alright, get some sleep. I'll be here when you wake up."

Teacher didn't respond. He fell asleep almost immediately.

•　　　•　　　•

As Teacher grew more ill, Konner became more determined to find some bobbin berries for him. Even if it was dangerous, Konner felt he had to take the chance. He couldn't just stand by and let Teacher die. He wasn't certain he could even find any, but he convinced himself he had to try.

One day, after Teacher fell asleep and all the cats were napping, Konner set out with a canteen full of water and no idea which direction might be best. He snuck away as quietly as he could so none of the cats would try to follow him, choosing the direction they were least likely to see him when he left.

He walked a long time, seeing neither bobbin bush nor ant nor much of any living thing other than sage and mesquite. There were hills on the horizon, so he turned toward them, hoping maybe to find a hidden water source. During their travels, they'd observed large stands of bobbin hedges close to ponds and streams. It made sense to him that's where they were more likely to grow.

He felt more assured with a destination in mind, as opposed to wandering aimlessly. He'd search the hills, spend as much time as he could, but promised himself he'd return before nightfall. He didn't want to leave Teacher alone for too long.

As he neared the base of the first rocky knoll, he searched the slopes for the bright green bobbins. He wasn't really watching where he was walking and almost stepped right into a column of ants. He'd come close, but apparently not close enough to distract them from whatever task they were about. They paid no attention to him.

The procession went in two directions. One was almost straight back the way he'd come. The other led deeper into the hills. He followed the latter, paralleling its path and never getting too close. He knew how dangerous swarms of the ants could be. If they changed direction, came after him, he'd have to run, hoping he wasn't running into more of them.

Watching carefully where he stepped, almost holding his breath as we went, it wasn't long before Konner let escape a sigh of relief. The ants had led him to a thicket of bobbins. They were the largest ones he'd ever seen, higher than his head and grown so close together they were like a wall. He guessed there must be water nearby, but he didn't care about that now. He just had to get close enough to pick some of the berries and get them back to Teacher.

There was a single large ant mound on one side of the hedge — that's where the column was headed, and where hundreds of other ants could be seen coming and going. So Konner circled around the opposite side, still watching where he stepped. He knew, despite the bustling activity around the mound, there could be ants anywhere.

As he approached the edge of the bobbin growth, he heard a strange sound. He thought it was just the wind until he got closer and saw a collection of hollowed-out stems atop the hedge of bobbins. There was no question in his mind that the whistling tune was coming from those stems, but the fact that what he heard was an uneven but recognizable melody astonished him. Not that he knew the specific tune as anything he'd heard before, but it definitely sounded like something of human origin. Because the sounds and their volume rose and fell with the wind, he was certain it was the gusts that powered the song. But he couldn't figure out how the variation of notes could possibly be created in such a harmonious pattern.

Then he saw something else — something that sent the shiver-tingles right through him. The extremities of various animals were half buried right up next to the stalks of the bushes. The tops of two rabbit ears poked out of the ground, along with what looked like a woodchuck's tail and possibly the hind legs of a dog or a ki-yote. There were no ants swarming on them as you might expect. Instead, they were just rotting, right up next to the bobbins, almost as if they were an offering.

The wind died down and the music it fed went silent. Cautiously, Konner continued closer, found some berries, and began plucking them and placing them in a small pouch he'd brought. He didn't think he needed many, but wanted to be sure he had enough to cure whatever it was that had made Teacher ill.

When he was satisfied he had plenty, he turned carefully to leave. Before he could take a step, he froze in place. Fear swept through his rigid form like a chill in the air. He was surrounded by a red swarm — more ants than he'd ever seen in one place. They'd fanned out across the ground in front of him, blanketing the area. There was nowhere for him to run. The bobbin thicket on one side, the ants spread across the other.

Konner held his breath. He didn't dare move. Even though it was apparent they were there to fence him in, he hoped against reason that if he didn't move, they might go away. They didn't. He wondered briefly if the music had summoned them, but he didn't know if ants could even hear.

For what seemed like forever, they didn't move at all. He kept expecting them to rush him, swarm him. He stood there, sweating, trying not to imagine what such a horrific death would be like. He fought against the terror, against a surging panic that shouted inside his brain, *Run!*

One grouping of ants abruptly moved away from the others. A score of the scarlet creatures, each almost the size of his little finger, marched toward him. But they stopped a few feet away. Konner was still afraid to move. He watched as the menacing bugs formed a line, following one after the other. The line began to curve and when they halted their march, they'd formed a circle — a perfect circle of ants.

Konner was dumbfounded. He looked down at the red ring, not sure of his own senses. His first thought was that it couldn't be real. He was seeing something that wasn't really there. Then the circle dissipated, and the ants reformed. He watched in amazement as the same group formed a square, five ants to a side.

Konner had no idea what they were doing. He only knew such behavior in any creature was amazing beyond words. He wondered if they were trying to communicate.

If so, what were they saying? How was he supposed to respond?

Konner took a chance. He bent down as slowly as he could. The ants didn't move.

Using his finger, he drew a square in the dirt, doing his best to approximate the size and perfection of the shape the ants had formed. When he finished, he stood back up. As he did, the squadron of ants reformed on the lines he'd dug into the ground.

For a minute that seemed to last for hours, the ants remained in the shape of his square. He had no idea what was next, so he waited. When minutes passed, he decided to try something else. He bent down again, and this time he drew a triangle into the soil. When he straightened up, the ants moved to his triangle and copied it exactly.

Because of its size, two of the ants were not needed to complete the three-sided shape. Instead, after seeming to inspect the border of the triangle, the two ants scurried off through the bobbins towards the mound on the other side of the thicket.

Konner waited. None of the ants in the triangle moved. Neither did the thousands spread out before him. They were waiting also. Waiting for what, Konner had no idea. But he also had no choice but to stand there. He was afraid the slightest move might be interpreted as a provocation.

While he never saw the two ants return, there was sudden activity. The ants forming the triangle moved off to join the giant swarm. Then, with no forewarning or signal he could recognize, the sea of ants before him parted. The wave of red moved several feet on each side, creating a pathway through them. Konner stood there, amazed once more, but he didn't stand still for long. While he struggled to comprehend what was happening — how it was happening==he knew this path was meant for him. Slowly, he moved onto it, warily watching the ants on either side as he went. He didn't run, he walked as calmly as he could, until he could no longer see any ants behind him.

Then he ran.

•   •   •

That night, after he'd had a chance to calm down, Konner thought about the ants. But the truth was, he didn't know what to think. To accept the little bugs were somehow intelligent defied everything he knew. But he didn't know how else could they have done what they did. And then to show him ... what? *Mercy?* They'd let him go when they easily could have killed him and buried him next to the bobbins like the other animals. *Why?* All because he drew a couple of shapes into the ground? Maybe it wasn't just the ants, thought Konner. Maybe Teacher had been right when he suggested the bobbin plants had changed them. Had they somehow modified the insects' brains? Had they made the ants more intelligent? Intelligent enough to understand geometric shapes? Or was it the bobbins themselves that were intelligent, and the ants were only following orders?

Konner found any of the possibilities difficult to believe. In all the things he'd read, only in fiction did anything come close to what he'd witnessed. But it wasn't fiction. He'd seen it with his own eyes. It had been real.

When Konner gave Teacher the bobbin berries, Teacher didn't say a word. He just stared at Konner for a moment with his rheumy gray eyes, then shook his head as if disappointed. He swallowed the handful of the purple berries as if to say, *They won't help, but since you went to the trouble.*

Konner wanted to tell him about his strange encounter with the ants, but he thought that might make Teacher even angrier with him. There was only silence between them for a long minute, then Teacher put his hand on Konner's arm.

"You know I'm dying, don't you, Konner?"

"But the berries might —"

"The berries won't help," he said harshly before Konner could finish. Then, more gently, he added, "There is no miracle cure, my boy. I'm beyond even the powers of the bobbin bush. I told you that, but you ... you were determined to help me, and I appreciate that. Even so, you need to be ready — to be smarter. You're going to be on your own soon. I don't know how long I have now. Not that any of us ever do. We're mortals all."

A tear ran down Konner's face. Teacher reached out and caught it with a fingertip.

"Don't cry, Konner. Crying does no good. What's important is remembering." He leaned back and looked straight up at nothing. "I remember when my father was dying, he made me promise not to let the words die with him — all the words in mankind's books. I kept my promise and now I've passed the words on to you. You're my legacy."

Another set of tears formed in Konner's eyes, but he quickly wiped them away.

"Are you .... are you afraid?"

Teacher chuckled. "You know what Mark Twain once said about that? He said, 'The fear of death follows from the fear of life. A man who lives fully is prepared to die at any time.' I've lived a strange life, Konner. Not the life my father or mother would have imagined for me, but I've lived it as fully as I could. As another writer once said, 'In the end we'll all become stories.' I've been part of many stories, so I can't complain. I'm part of your story, and you're part of mine. Someday you'll have dozens of your own stories."

Konner nodded and said, "I'm glad you were part of mine. There's so much I wouldn't have learned without you."

"And I was glad to be your teacher."

Konner thought about how the old fellow had been more than just his teacher. He'd been like a father — the father Konner had once had but lost.

"There's one thing I've always wanted to ask you."

"Well there's no time like the present."

"What's your name — your real name?"

"My name?" Teacher paused for a few seconds. Whether he was remembering or just trying to form the sounds in his mouth, Konner wasn't sure. "In another life, my name was Adam."

•   •   •

Adam, whom Konner knew for so long as "Teacher," died that night. When Konner found him in the morning, Gollum was lying lifeless by his master's side. Konner didn't know which of them had gone first, but he hoped they'd gone together.

He spent half a day digging a hole. After he managed to get Teacher in it, he placed Gollum on top of him. The other cats had taken turns smelling the bodies, but didn't react otherwise. Konner figured they accepted the loss of their friends as a natural part of life.

Konner himself was not so accepting. He looked down at the corpses, hesitant to cover them. He put his hands in his pockets and felt his goldstone, which he'd kept all these years. He no longer believed in luck, or in any "superstitious nonsense" as Teacher used to call it. In a sudden fit of anger, he pulled out the stone and made to throw it as far away as he could. But something stopped him. Instead of throwing it, he dropped it into the hole with Teacher and Gollum.

He knew he'd have to cover them up soon, but he felt like he should say something first. He had no idea of what he should say, until he remembered something from his past.

"The earth is the land, and we are the earth."

AUTHOR'S NOTE

"Enlightenment" is part of a longer apocalyptic novel Bruce Golden is putting together titled *After the End*, about what happens to the Earth after a comet collides with the planet, killing off most of humanity.

ABOUT THE AUTHOR

Bruce Golden has sold more than a hundred short stories published across a score of countries and three dozen anthologies. His recent novella, *Monster Town*, a satirical take on the world of the hard-boiled detective — one populated by the monsters of old black and white horror movies — is in development as a television series.

YOU MIGHT ALSO ENJOY

DENISOVAN HARMONY
by DJ Cockburn

You're watching the first Homo denisova to walk the earth in a hundred and fifty centuries grope their way into adolescence.

GIFT OF SILENCE
by Alfred Smith

Mara's son is at the center of her burning city and his song out of control. She may not be able to save them both.

GREY MOTHER MOUNTAIN
by Elyse Russell

When her village is destroyed, an elderly woman seeks help from the last remaining dragon to get revenge.

Available in digital and trade paperback editions from
Water Dragon Publishing
waterdragonpublishing.com